Adventures of John and Jaya

COOKING IN THE KITCHEN

Felicia Denise

ILLUSTRATED BY JOHN JR.

Printed and bound in the United States of America

First Printing, 2017

ISBN 978-1979247863

ISBN 1979247862

Dedication

I'd like to dedicate this book to the most important people in my life...my family!

More specifically, I'd like to dedicate this book to my son and daughter. They are after all the reason I wrote the book. My daughter's spunky and colorful personality really made her character come alive in this book. Thanks for giving me a plethora of material to work with! My son's levelheadedness really embodies the role of a big brother. Thanks for being my illustrator.

To watch their funny antics and to see how they have grown has brought my husband and I much joy and pride! I am excited to be able to share a glimpse of our life with you!

My dedications wouldn't be complete if I failed to mention my husband, my mom, my sister, and my nephew, but more importantly my dad who left this world knowing I had written a book but, never saw it come to fruition. Here's to you Daddy...I did it!

John and Jaya are brother and sister. They love taking adventures.

"Adventure begins!" exclaims John. "Where will our adventure take us today?"

"In the kitchen," says Jaya. "Good, that's not far away," said John. "Let's bake a cake for Daddy while he's visiting our Aunt Faye."

"Great!" says Jaya. "I love to cook." She grabs the mixing bowl and spoon while John begins reading the directions out of their Mommy's favorite cookbook. "Jaya, the directions say, to make cake pour mix, crack eggs, blend, and bake."

"That's easy," says Jaya with a grin. "I've poured the mix, cracked the eggs, but wait. Should the shells go in?"

"NO!" replies John with a puzzled look on his face. So, Jaya finishes mixing and gives him a taste.

She asks....

"Was it yummy, was it great, did it blow your mind? John, have you ever tasted something so sweet, so delicious, and divine?"

John smiles and gives his sister a wink!

Next, Jaya asks, "Do we pour it in a bowl, serve it with a spoon and... "No way!" John interrupts. "Little sis, we have one more important step we must take. If we skip this one, it will be pudding that we'll make!"

"What's the last step already?" Jaya says impatiently. "I can't take it anymore!" "Tell me, tell me!"

Her brother replies, "With Mommy's help, pour the mix in a pan, put it in the oven, and close the door. Right before your eyes, wait for it, wait for it. Then it magically will rise!"

Now they can see from the oven door window that the cake is golden brown. "It's ready, it's ready!" the children screech. "Mommy, please come down!" But, wouldn't you know it, Mom cannot be found.

"How will we take it out of the oven?" cries Jaya. "It's going to burn!" They both start to worry and can't help but fuss. "Our cake is going to burn. Will someone please help us?"

Just then, down the stairs, Mommy flies into the kitchen. She swoops down to save the day. Mommy opens the oven and places the cake on the cooling tray.

"Thanks Mom!" John and Jaya scream with relief.

"Now here's the hard part Jaya, I forgot to tell you," says John. "What?" Jaya replies, frightened to hear. "We have to wait twenty minutes for the cake to cool," says John."

"Twenty minutes, that's too long. It sounds like forever!" cries Jaya.

"It won't take that long. Let's sit and wait together," says John.

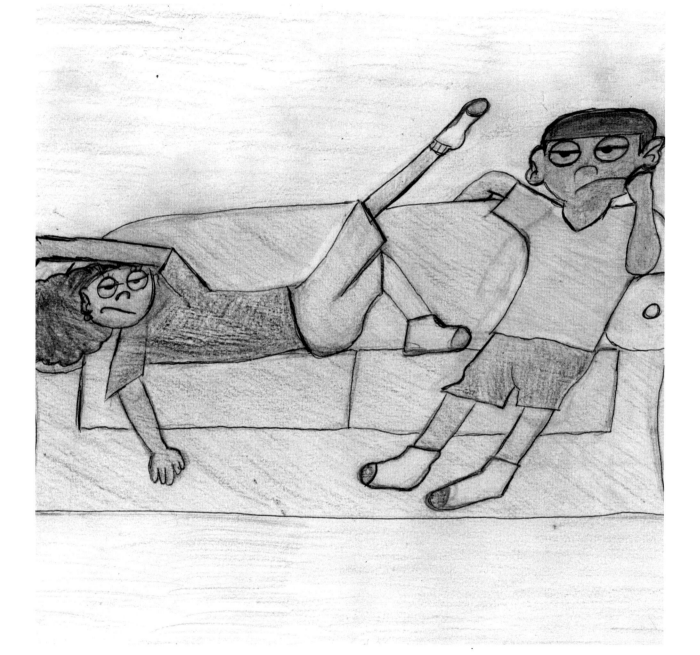

After their wait is through, Jaya asks John, "Do we have to wait for Daddy too? We've waited so long. Now what should we do?"

John looks at his sister and can tell she is sad. "Let's cut the cake in half, saving some for Mom and some for Dad."

"Good idea!" agrees his sister.

Then Jaya says, "Let's call Mom to cut the cake, and give her a taste to see if she thinks it's great!" So, the children call their Mom. "Mommy, Mommy you have to see! The cake is frosted. Can you cut it for me?" "Alright dears, here I come," Mom replies. "Let's cut the cake and have some fun!"

"Jaya, let Mommy taste a tiny bite," John says. "Okay Mom, what do you think?"

As the children wait for Mommy's answer the anticipation is too much. Jaya blurts out,

"Is it yummy, is it great, does it blow your mind? Mommy have you ever tasted something so sweet, so delicious, and divine?"

But before Mommy can take a bite.

Daddy opens the front door.

The children scream, "You're home, you're home! We have a special treat. Now sit and relax in your favorite seat. Sit down, sit down! Let's eat!"

So Daddy takes his seat and listens to his children tell all about the adventures they had in the kitchen today. John asks, "Daddy, how was Aunt Faye?"

Jaya interrupts, "Daddy, Daddy, take a bite of our cake. We made it for you and I simply just can't wait!"

Knowing his daughter cannot wait, Daddy dug in and finished his plate.

Once Daddy finishes, Jaya yells...

"Was it yummy, was it great, did it blow your mind? Daddy, have you ever tasted something so sweet, so delicious, and divine?"

John and Jaya's Dad smiles and says, "This cake is delicious, and boy you were right. Kids you've done a great job. But I can't take another bite! *Yummy*!"

Kids, here is a simple cake recipe you can make with your Mommy and Daddy. Enjoy!

John & Jaya's Cake Recipe

Ingredients:

1 cup white sugar

1/2 cup butter (room temperature)

2 eggs

2 1/2 teaspoons vanilla extract

1 1/2 cups all-purpose flour

1 3/4 teaspoons baking powder

1/2 cup of buttermilk

Directions:

- Preheat oven to 350 degrees F (175 degrees C). Grease and flour a 9x9 inch pan.

- In a medium bowl, cream together the sugar and butter. Beat in the eggs, one at a time, then stir in the vanilla. Combine flour and baking powder. Add to the creamed mixture and mix well. Finally, stir in the milk until batter is smooth. Pour or spoon batter into the prepared pan.

- Bake for 30 to 40 minutes in the preheated oven. Cake is done when it springs back to the touch.

"Was it yummy, was it great, did it blow your mind? Kids have you ever tasted something so sweet, so delicious, and divine?"